YO-DOI-128

MATH ADVENTURES

AVA VISITS THE AQUARIUM

AN ODDS AND EVENS ADVENTURE

by Megan Atwood
illustrated by Amy Zhing

Tools for Parents & Teachers

Grasshopper Books enhance imagination and introduce the earliest readers to fiction with fun storylines and illustrations. The easy-to-read text supports early reading experiences with repetitive sentence patterns and sight words.

Before Reading

- Look at the cover illustration. What do readers see? What do they think the book will be about?

- Look at the picture glossary together. Sound out the words. Ask readers to identify the first letter of each vocabulary word.

Read the Book

- "Walk" through the book, reading to or along with the reader. Point to the illustrations as you read.

After Reading

- Review the picture glossary again. Ask readers to locate the words in the text.

- Ask the reader: What is your favorite number? Is it an even number or an odd number? How do you know?

Grasshopper Books are published by Jump!
5357 Penn Avenue South
Minneapolis, MN 55419
www.jumplibrary.com

Copyright © 2022 Jump! International copyright reserved in all countries. No part of this book may be reproduced in any form without written permission from the publisher.

Library of Congress Cataloging-in-Publication Data

Names: Atwood, Megan, author. | Zhing, Amy, illustrator.
Title: Ava visits the aquarium: an odds and evens adventure / by Megan Atwood; illustrated by Amy Zhing.
Description: Minneapolis, MN: Jump!, Inc., [2022]
Series: Math adventures
Audience: Ages 4-7.
Identifiers: LCCN 2021038121 (print)
LCCN 2021038122 (ebook)
ISBN 9781636906232 (hardcover)
ISBN 9781636906249 (paperback)
ISBN 9781636906256 (ebook)
Subjects: LCSH: Readers (Primary)
Numbers, Natural–Juvenile fiction.
LCGFT: Readers (Publications)
Classification: LCC PE1119.2.A8926 2022 (print)
LCC PE1119.2 (ebook) | DDC 428.6/2–dc23
LC record available at https://lccn.loc.gov/2021038121
LC ebook record available at https://lccn.loc.gov/2021038122

Editor: Eliza Leahy
Direction and Layout: Anna Peterson
Illustrator: Amy Zhing

Printed in the United States of America at Corporate Graphics in North Mankato, Minnesota.

Table of Contents

Animal Pairs

"Class, please get into pairs," says Mr. Li.

Ava counts eight other kids.

That makes nine total.

5

"I can't make a pair," Ava says.

"Oh, that's right. There are nine students. Nine is an odd number. It can't be split into pairs. We will have one group of three!" Mr. Li says.

Ava joins Joe and Nate.

They watch the fish.

Three swim by.

Three is an odd number.

Next, they see three dolphins.

The dolphins smile.

10

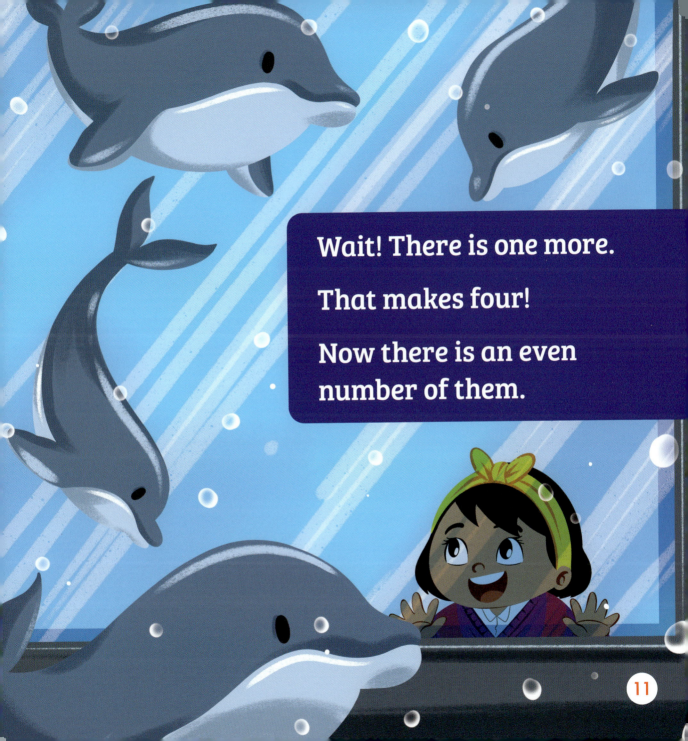

Wait! There is one more.

That makes four!

Now there is an even number of them.

Ava loves sea stars.

She counts five.

Each one has five arms.

Five is an odd number.

13

Ava sees an octopus.

It has eight arms.

That is four pairs of two.

"I only have one pair of arms," Ava says. "That is two. Eight and two are even numbers!"

Let's Review!

Flip to page 5. How many fish can you count? Is it an odd or even number?

A. 7   **B.** 8   **C.** 9   **D.** 10

Picture Glossary

even number
A number that can be divided evenly by two.

odd number
A number that cannot be divided evenly by two.

pairs
Groups of two.

total
Making up the whole amount.